THIS OUT-OF-THIS-WORLD
BOOK BELONGS TO

_____

Published by Scholastic Inc., 90 Old Sherman Turnpike, Danbury, Connecticut 06816.

For information regarding permission, write to:
Disney Licensed Publishing, 114 Fifth Avenue, New York, New York 10011.

978-0-545-08625-7   0-545-08625-6
Printed in the U.S.A.   First printing, May 2008

DISNEY · PIXAR

WALL·E

SCHOLASTIC INC.

New York   Toronto   London   Auckland   Sydney
Mexico City   New Delhi   Hong Kong   Buenos Aires

Earth was a lonely place in the year 2805. It was also a dirty place. Humans left the planet 700 years ago after it became too polluted. They left behind towers of trash. They also left behind a robot named WALL•E, which stands for Waste Allocation Load Lifter—Earth class. WALL•E's job was to compact the garbage into cubes.

As he worked each day, WALL•E found all sorts of treasures— old toys, a lightbulb, even an eggbeater.

Each day after work, WALL•E returned to the old truck he called home. He would stash away the treasures he found and then turn on his favorite movie. Although he had a pet cockroach to keep him company, WALL•E was very lonely. He dreamed of being in love and holding hands with someone.

One morning, WALL•E went to work as he always did and began cubing trash. On this particular day, though, his life would change.

The robot discovered something he had never seen before—a plant. WALL•E didn't know what it was. He lifted it carefully, put it in an old boot, and took it home.

Not very long after, a spaceship landed and out popped a shiny sleek robot. Her name was EVE; and for WALL•E, it was love at first sight.

Once she landed, EVE began searching for something. WALL•E secretly followed her. Finally, the two met.

"Eee-vah," WALL•E repeated, mispronouncing the most beautiful name he had ever heard.

A few moments later, a terrible sandstorm hit. To escape, WALL•E took EVE to his home. WALL•E was truly happy for the first time. He showed off all his fine treasures. Then he played his favorite movie for her. EVE giggled as WALL•E danced to the music from the movie.

When EVE tried dancing, she spun so fast that she broke a few of WALL•E's things—including one of his eyes! Luckily, the robotic treasure-hunter had lots of spare parts.

The fun ended when WALL•E showed EVE the strange little green thing he had put in the boot. EVE immediately froze. A hidden compartment on her chest opened and a beam of light shot out. The light took hold of the plant and moved it towards the opening in EVE's chest.

Once the plant was inside of her, EVE completely shut down. The only thing that seemed to work was a flashing green light.

13

WALL•E didn't know what to do. He tried to wake EVE up. He tapped her gently. "Eee-vah?" he said sadly.

EVE didn't move at all. WALL•E tried everything to bring EVE back to life. He recharged her in the morning sunlight.

He took EVE for walks and boat rides.

He shielded her from the afternoon rain.

Nothing worked.

EVE stayed shut down.

One day, the spaceship returned to Earth to pick up EVE. WALL•E was now faced with a life-changing decision: Stay on Earth or go with EVE? WALL•E said good-bye to his pet cockroach and followed his mechanical heart.

He held on tightly to the spaceship as it blasted into space.

WALL•E had never been in space before. It was full of wonders. "Oooooo!" he said as he gazed at the twinkling stars, the rings of Saturn, and the amazing view of Earth.

WALL•E clung desperately to the spaceship as it headed towards a massive star liner called the *Axiom*, the pride of the Buy n Large fleet. The ship housed a city full of people. Buy n Large was the superstore that had controlled Earth. The company's CEO had promised to clean up Earth while the people were away. That was more than 700 years ago and not much had changed.

17

After the ship docked with the *Axiom*, WALL•E secretly followed as steward-bots escorted EVE aboard the *Axiom*. EVE's green light continued to flash. That meant there was a plant inside her.

On the bridge, the ship's electronic Autopilot, or Auto, inspected EVE. Auto did most of the Captain's work and wanted to be in charge.

As Auto continued to examine EVE, she woke up!

WALL•E was quietly hiding nearby. When he saw EVE spring to life, WALL•E gasped in robotic amazement. "Eee-vah!" he whispered.

EVE was surprised to see the little robot. She motioned for him to be quiet.

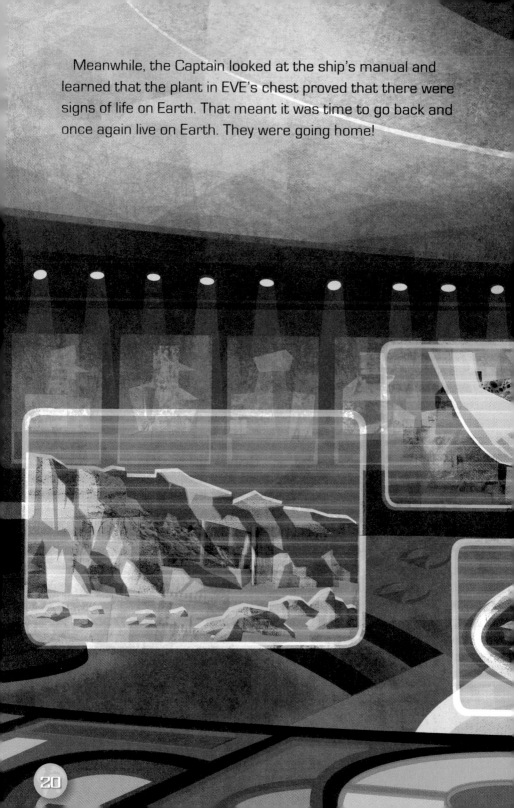

Meanwhile, the Captain looked at the ship's manual and learned that the plant in EVE's chest proved that there were signs of life on Earth. That meant it was time to go back and once again live on Earth. They were going home!

The plant needed to be placed in the ship's holo-detector. The holo-detector would then spin the ship around and head back to Earth. But when EVE's chest cavity opened, the plant was gone! The Captain ordered Auto to scan EVE to see if she still had the plant.

"Probe memory is faulty," Auto reported.

"Send her to the repair ward," instructed the Captain. Then he went back to the manual to learn all about Earth. As for WALL•E— the repair-bots came and got him.

In the repair ward, the ship's repair-bots placed WALL•E with
a bunch of broken down reject-bots. But WALL•E kept his eye on
EVE. When the repair-bots took off EVE's blaster arm to clean it,
WALL•E thought they were hurting her.

WALL•E struggled to free himself and crashed through the glass doors. He grabbed EVE's blaster arm, accidentally shooting out the repair ward control panel. Suddenly the doors to the repair ward opened. The mob of reject-bots cheered wildly. They were free! They lifted WALL•E onto their shoulders. WALL•E was a hero.
   Everyone escaped.

Word spread instantly. All over the *Axiom* came the warning: "Caution: Rogue Robots." The steward-bots tried to recapture the robots. But the reject-bots fought them off as EVE and WALL•E escaped. Images of WALL•E and EVE appeared on holo-screens all over the ship.

As WALL•E moved through the ship, he saw a number of people riding by in hover chairs. The humans had no reason to move. Everything was done for them. The humans stared straight ahead at the floating holo-screens in front of them. They never got out of their chairs.

WALL•E and EVE frantically ran from the steward-bots, hiding in the bay of the escape-pod. They secretly watched as GO-4, Auto's assistant, appeared.

Under orders from Auto, GO-4 had taken the plant from Eve, and put it in the escape pod. GO-4 planned to launch the plant into outer space! Without the plant, the ship could not return to Earth.

But WALL•E sneaked into the pod to retrieve the plant—just as GO-4 launched the pod into space!

"Eeee!" screamed WALL•E. He pushed every button to try to stop the pod. Then he pushed the wrong button.

"Pod will self-destruct in ten seconds," the computer announced.

WALL•E frantically looked around. Then he spotted something that just might save him.

In the meantime, EVE had followed WALL•E into space.

WALL•E thought fast and hard. Before the pod exploded, he grabbed a fire extinguisher, got out of the pod, pulled the pin, and with a terrific *whoosh*, he zoomed out into space and past EVE.

EVE raced to catch up with him. When she did, WALL•E showed her the plant. He had saved it. Delighted, EVE rested her head against WALL•E's. A spark of electricity passed between them—a robot kiss.

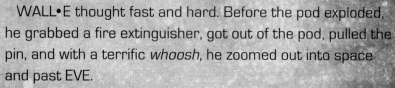

Once they were back inside the *Axiom*, EVE delivered the plant to the Captain. She then projected the images that she had recorded on Earth. For the first time, EVE saw how WALL•E had lovingly cared for her while she was shut down. She also saw WALL•E's desire to hold her hand. Eve was touched.

As the Captain watched the images EVE had recorded, he became excited about returning to Earth.

The head of Buy n Large had long ago decided to keep humans in space forever. Auto had orders to prevent the *Axiom* from returning to Earth.

Refusing the Captain's order to turn on the holo-detector, Auto instructed GO-4 to grab the plant and throw it down the garbage chute. Luckily, WALL•E caught it and brought it back to the bridge.

The Captain was thrilled until—**ZAP!**

Auto jolted WALL•E with a blast of electricity. The robot fell to the floor and couldn't move.

Banished to the garbage depot, EVE felt horrible as she gazed at WALL•E's broken parts. She held out her hand to WALL•E— to grant his wish to hold her hand. WALL•E mustered enough strength and handed her the plant instead. It was at that moment that EVE realized she didn't care about her mission anymore. She cared only about WALL•E.

"Errr," muttered WALL•E, trying to say Earth. For EVE to fix WALL•E, they had to return to his truck on Earth where the little bot kept spare parts. It was up to EVE to get the *Axiom* back to Earth. **KABOOM!** She blasted a hole through the wall of the garbage depot and zoomed out.

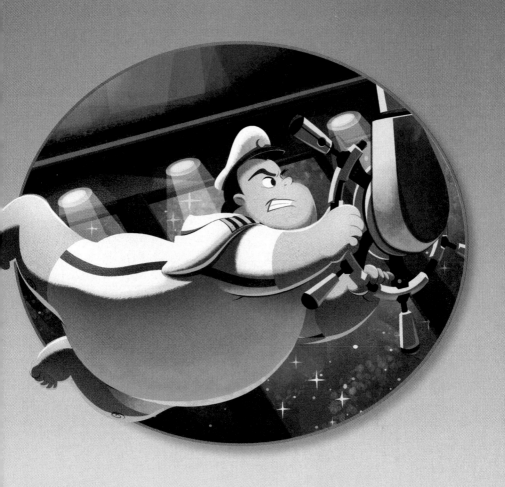

Back on the bridge, Auto and the Captain were locked in a fierce battle, as the Captain tried to regain control of the ship. During their struggle, the Captain managed to hit the holo-detector button, activating it.

WALL•E and EVE arrived at the lido deck and saw the holo-detector rising. Then to their horror, it started sinking. Auto had deactivated it! WALL•E acted quickly and bravely. Although still injured from his earlier battle with Auto, the little robot jammed himself under the detector to stop its descent.

From the bridge, the Captain watched and knew it was time for drastic measures: He actually stood up! Then the Captain walked over to Auto and turned off its power switch.

"You are hereby relieved of duty," the Captain said, as he shut Auto off.

On the lido deck, EVE put the plant inside the holo-detector. "Plant origin verified. Set course for Earth," said the computer. Then the holo-detector lifted off of WALL•E. He collapsed on the floor, crushed and broken. EVE sadly cradled him in her arms.

Finally, the *Axiom* landed on Earth. EVE whisked WALL•E to his home and began to repair him, as the reject robots watched. When EVE was done, she blasted a hole in the roof. Sunlight poured in. The sun's life-giving rays recharged WALL•E.

WALL•E sprung back to life. EVE was thrilled. She held out her hand, but WALL•E just stared at it. Then he began compacting all the treasures he had found as if they were trash. He seemed not to remember anything about his life with EVE.

EVE couldn't believe it. Frustrated, she shook the little robot, but it was no use. WALL•E continued to do his job. Heartbroken, EVE leaned in towards him and took the tiny robot's hand.

"WALL•E?" she said. A spark of energy passed between the two.

WALL•E suddenly moved his hands as his eyes began to focus and light up. "Eee-vah?"

EVE was thrilled. WALL•E had returned to her!

Meanwhile, the passengers had filed out of the ship. They took in the sunlight and looked around at Earth. The Captain had found a spot of dirt and dug a hole. Then he gently placed the plant in the ground.

WALL•E and EVE had helped bring life back to Earth and had also found each other. As the sun set, they sat together, holding hands.

3...2...1...

Blast off to the future and find these pictures.